The
PILGRIM'S PROGRESS

Christian meets Hopeful. [*Page* 89]

The
PILGRIM'S PROGRESS

Specially rewritten for children by
Laurence G. S. Morris
from John Bunyan's original

CHRISTIAN ❖ LITERATURE ❖ CRUSADE
Fort Washington, Pennsylvania 19034

CHRISTIAN LITERATURE CRUSADE

U.S.A.
P.O. Box 1449, Fort Washington, PA 19034

with publishing programs also in:
GREAT BRITAIN
51 The Dean, Alresford, Hants. SO24 9BJ

AUSTRALIA
P.O. Box 419M, Manunda, QLD 4879

NEW ZEALAND
10 MacArthur Street, Feilding

ISBN 0-87508-747-7

Copyright © 1954
Laurence G. S. Morris

This printing 1999

Printed in the United States of America

ILLUSTRATIONS

FOREWORD

There once lived in the village of Elstow, England a poor man who earned his living by mending pots and pans. He was known to most people who lived in those parts as the tinker, and his name was John Bunyan.

Through the streets and lanes of the villages of Bedfordshire he could be seen pushing his old barrow, and as he journeyed he would cry, "Any old pots to mend—knives to grind?" In those far-off days it was not easy for the poor people to buy new utensils, for they were scarce and very expensive. John was kept very busy and his work took him to most of the villages as well as the county town of Bedford, where he was a familiar figure with the inhabitants.

The tinker had been a careless boy, being prone to all kinds of mischief, which, although not thoroughly wicked, had caused his parents many anxious moments. They had spent much of their hard-earned money on his education, sending him to the Grammar School, where he received good training in the "three R's"—reading, writing, and arithmetic. The knowledge he gained there stood him in good stead later on in life.

9

When he left school he made friends with some of the coarser lads of the village, and John, like them, became a nuisance and was often in trouble. In his heart he was ashamed of his unseemly behavior, and many times he intended to turn over a new leaf, but his companions soon dragged him down again and caused him to commit more follies. In his early teens he fell in love with a gentle maiden who was as beautiful as she was good. She made John promise to forsake his companions and try to live a better life. A year or so later the two married and lived in a little cottage in the village where John was brought up. But all his promises to his dear wife were broken, and he soon found his delights among his old companions again. Mrs. Bunyan was troubled about her husband and implored him to give up his friends and wayward habits. At last he agreed.

During one of his frequent visits to Bedford, John overheard an interesting conversation between two ladies who were looking into a big Book. They were speaking with great sincerity and raised their voices, so that the tinker could not help hearing their conversation.

"What a wonderful Book this is to be sure!" said the one to the other. "It gives us instruction in the Ways of God, and shows how we can live a good and honest life in a world where there is much to distress and cause us harm."

"Yes, indeed," replied the other lady. "I have found help and encouragement in its precious pages during many long years. The Book not only guides us in this life, but also it points to a life that is eternal in Heaven."

At this point John interrupted and said: "You will think that I am very rude, listening to your conversation, but I am deeply interested and would like to hear more about this Book of which you speak.'' He had left his barrow and was standing near the two friends.

''This volume is called the Holy Bible and we know it to be the Word of God,'' replied one of the friends. ''There are many passages in it that are hard to understand, but the gospel story and numerous precious promises found within its pages are proof that the Creator has inspired them.''

''I agree with my friend,'' added the other lady, ''and the more I read this Book the more enchanted I become with its thrilling stories.''

The tinker pondered these words and promised to commence a serious study of the Bible. Many people make promises only to break them, but John was not like that, for he quickly obtained a Bible and began to read it with great interest. At first he found it difficult to understand some of the stories, but as he continued to read he began to learn of Jesus and His love. The effect this had on his way of life was amazing; whereas he had once found his pleasure among bad companions he now found new friends, and went about the villages telling everyone about this wonderful Book.

At that time John began to preach to large numbers of people on the village green. A great change had come over him, for he had become a Christian and many of the villagers were persuaded to become Christians too.

The people of Bunyan's day were very ignorant. Schools were expensive luxuries, and only a few people were able to read. The crowds that assembled to hear the Scriptures were ordinary villagers and they listened to the Good News for the first time. It was not long before Bunyan began to receive invitations to preach in towns far distant from Elstow. Everywhere he went the people gladly heard him. This aroused the jealousy of certain religious leaders, who tried to stop him. "If we allow this fellow to teach the people," remarked one, "he will eventually oust us from our pulpits; indeed, we have already noticed that our churches are less full, and this state of affairs must stop."

Now it was a serious offense to cause discontent among the parishioners, and although John Bunyan was not guilty of such an offense, wicked men falsely accused him before the magistrates. He was committed for trial and found guilty, and sentenced to a term of twelve years' imprisonment in Bedford Prison. John had many friends who tried to procure his release, but they were unsuccessful.

The prison was situated by the River Ouse and his cell was uncomfortably damp. It was sparsely furnished with a hard couch, a rickety table, and a chair. Bunyan earned a small income by fastening metal bindings on the ends of boot laces in order to provide food for his wife and his four small children.

When the day's work was over, Bunyan, alone in his cell, would settle himself on his rough couch and study the Bible. Often his head would nod and he would fall asleep with the Book on his lap; at such times he dreamed and pictured himself in a beautiful land where there were no prisons but many mansions.

One night the tinker lay on his bed thinking about the unhappy condition of his many friends—their poverty and their burdens—and fell asleep. As he slept he dreamed that a man dressed in rags was carrying a heavy load on his back.

John Bunyan in prison.

From this the man was unable to free himself, though he tried with much toil and pain. A Book was in his hand and, as he read it, he cried out, "What must I do to be saved?" John, in his dream, followed this man, whose name was Christian, through many strange and wonderful adventures. When he awoke he recorded these stories and later formed them into the book that was to make his name famous—*The Pilgrim's Progress.*

Since the first edition was published, many millions of copies have been sold, and, translated into numerous languages, have found their way into almost every Christian home throughout the world.

There are, however, many who think that the original allegory is not only too long but in places difficult to follow. These pages retell some of the most interesting stories in simple language for young children, and it is hoped that with the beautiful illustrations this children's edition of *The Pilgrim's Progress* will meet with a good reception.

ONE

There lived once in a certain large city a poor man who was very unhappy because he carried a heavy load on his back and could not by any means get rid of it. He visited a number of people who said they were able to remove burdens, but however much they tried, they were unable to remove his. At night he would try to forget his trouble in sleep, but then strange dreams came to his mind, and he awakened with great fear. In this way he would lie on his bed, longing for the morning to come. (Boys and girls sometimes find it difficult to get to sleep, especially if they are not feeling well. How glad they are when Mother brings a soothing drink—that soon drives away the pain. The man in our story, however, could not be comforted in this way, because his pain was different from any that is usually felt.)

"What must I do to get rid of this heavy load?" he would cry. His wife and children were very distressed to see him in such trouble, and they told him to try to forget his burden. He would walk by himself in the fields, reading a Book which he always carried, and, strange as it may seem, his burden became heavier as he read.

One morning he was walking somewhat farther than usual from the city when he saw a man coming toward him, who appeared to be very gentle and kind. He was a stranger and was not like the people who dwelt in those parts. The townsfolk were mostly dressed in bright colors, and it was therefore easy to see that this man had come from another town, because his clothes were differently made and more in keeping with his noble bearing. He appeared to be a true gentleman, and it was his kind expression that caused the troubled man to take notice of him.

"You're looking very unhappy," observed the stranger; "what is your trouble and why are you carrying such a heavy load?"

"Sir, I have been reading from this Book, and it tells me I am a great sinner and deserve to be punished; this causes me to feel the tremendous weight of my sins and I cannot bear them much longer."

Thus the weary man told the stranger of his terrible troubles.

"What is your name?" asked the gentleman.

"Christian," replied our friend. "But I am wrongly so called, for I do not follow Christ."

The kind man was very sorry to see the unhappy condition of Christian, and he comforted him with the news that he had been sent by the king to give him help and advice.

"Thank you very much," replied the burdened one. "I will listen carefully to what you have to say."

"You want to be rid of your heavy load and you have tried every means, but as yet have failed. I can tell you where it can be removed; but before this happens you will have to

follow my direction. Do you see that gate in the distance?"
He was pointing to a small lodge-gate away on the horizon.

"No," replied Christian, "but I can see a light."

"Well," said Evangelist (for that was the stranger's
name), "make your way toward that light and you will then
arrive at the gate, where you will be given further
instructions."

"Thank you very much, kind sir," said Christian, hope
dawning in his face. He received from the stranger a
parchment scroll on which were written the words: *Flee
from the Wrath to Come*. "Show this scroll to the porter
who opens the lodge-gate, and he will then allow you to
enter." Thus Evangelist instructed Christian, and then bade
him farewell.

The poor man understood the strange words on the
parchment to mean that the city in which he lived was going
to be stricken with terrible trouble, and he was to run away
from it before it was too late. He therefore returned to his
home and warned his family and friends, imploring them to
come away with him. "If you remain here you will cause
untold suffering to yourself and the dear children." This he
said to his wife, and added, "I do love you all very much and
want you to enjoy the blessings that are to be ours when we
have finished the journey. The good Evangelist has told me
that if we are prepared to leave this wicked city and go on
pilgrimage, we shall receive forgiveness for all our sins and
come at last to a land where there is fullness of joy. It is a
City where all are happy; where there is no pain nor heavy
burdens, nor anything that will mar our everlasting bliss.
The Lord Jesus is the King of the land, and He waits to

receive all who will come to Him.'' In this way Christian sought to persuade his dear ones to accompany him on pilgrimage; but they would not listen to him and thought that his trouble had at last turned his brain.

''We do not believe such silly stories,'' replied his wife, ''and I am not going to risk the children's happiness by letting them go with you on pilgrimage.

''Why have you grown dissatisfied with your home?'' she continued. ''The pleasures of our lovely city are many and you used to enjoy them to the full.''

''That is true,'' replied her husband, ''but I have learned that the pleasures of this city are not to be compared with the happiness that awaits those who reach the Celestial City. *There are Pleasures Untold in that City of Gold.''*

''Enough of this nonsense,'' exclaimed the dear lady. ''It is very foolish to give up all the lovely things that are to be found here in order that you may enjoy uncertain blessings at some future time. Who has seen this strange land? It is possible that the man called Evangelist is mistaken. He may even be deceiving you,'' she added.

''I cannot believe that of him,'' replied Christian, ''for he appeared to be a man of truth and the description of the Celestial City is to be found in the Book that I have been reading.''

''Have you considered the hazards of such a journey? There will be many pitfalls, many hardships, and you may be unable to reach the City because of the difficulties.''

''I have considered the many trials that I shall have to undergo, but feel sure that the King of that country will send His servants to help me in the Way.'' Christian began to see that it would be useless to continue the conversation with his wife, for she had fully made up her mind to stay in the city.

"If you will not come with me, then I must go alone," he told her. "I cannot remain here, and my burden is so heavy that I must go to the place where it can be taken from me."

He kissed his wife and children good-bye, and with many a heartache started on his journey. Before he left the City of Destruction, two men joined him and asked him why he was leaving his family and friends. Christian told them of his deep need—to free himself from the heavy burden that was so tightly fastened to his back—and the news that the city in which they lived was to receive a terrible judgment.

"Will you accompany me on my journey?" added the pilgrim.

"What!" exclaimed one of the men, whose name was Obstinate. "And leave our friends and our comforts behind us?"

"Yes, certainly," replied Christian, "because the joys that you will gain by becoming pilgrims will be much deeper than any so-called pleasures you now experience. Come away, and prove my words to be true."

"What are the things you seek, since you leave all the world to find them?"

"I seek a City that is lovely beyond compare: the people who live there are forever happy. They have no need of the passing pleasures of this country, for they possess riches beyond our wildest dreams. You can read about the City in this Book." He offered Obstinate the volume so that he could read it for himself.

"Tush!" said Obstinate. "Away with your Book: will

you go back with us or no?"

"Never! How can I return now? It would mean that my burden would remain on my back forever, and I should be in the city when disaster overtakes it."

"Come then, neighbor Pliable" (for that was Obstinate's friend's name), "let us turn again and go home without him. There are many like this crazy pilgrim, who when they get an idea into their heads are wiser than seven men who can explain their doings."

Then said Pliable, "don't be rude to our friend; if what he says is true, the things he is going after are better than the things that we have. I feel inclined to journey with him on pilgrimage."

"What, are you also mad? Come back to the city with me before it is too late." Obstinate tried to persuade his companion to return with him, but he was unsuccessful.

He therefore went back to his townsfolk alone and told them how foolish Pliable was to listen to Christian. "He will find that the Pilgrim Way is too hard and before long we shall see him again. I do not think he has the courage to face all the dangers of the road."

Christian was delighted to have a companion who was willing to travel with him on the difficult journey.

You will remember that the pilgrim was making his way to the lodge-gate, but he was unable to see it. He knew he was on the right road because Evangelist had told him to keep the light before his eyes, and he could just see it on the distant horizon.

Pliable took his arm and they journeyed along together.

"Can I give you an account of some of the vast treasures

that are to be found in the Celestial City?'' said Christian presently. ''I am told that the streets are made of pure gold; pearls and other precious stones are there in abundance and there is a marvelous light shining all the time.''

''Isn't there any nighttime, then?'' asked Pliable wonderingly.

''No, there is no night there, neither is there any need of the sun, for the King is the Light of the City.''

''Oh, it will be wonderful to enter such a City.''

Poor Pliable was unable to understand much of Christian's conversation. ''How can a country have no nighttime?'' he thought.

Thus they spoke one with the other and thus they journeyed.

The City of Destruction was now far behind them, and as they turned their heads back to see, it had almost faded from view. The people who were still living there were busy about their work and pleasures, and had little time to think about Christian and Pliable.

Christian's wife must have felt sad at losing her husband, but she found plenty to do and tried not to remember her folly in not going with him. The pilgrim could not forget her and he prayed to God, asking Him to take care of her and the children. He hoped that she would follow after him at some future time.

The two friends had now walked a considerable way, and Christian thought that he could just make out the gate through which they were to pass. There was very little to interest them on the road, and the burden on his back made the going rather slow.

21

"I would like you to tell me more about our pilgrimage," said Pliable, who walked just a little in front of the poor burdened one. He had ceased to help Christian along, for he found that his arm was heavy upon him.

"Evangelist told me that I should be given further instructions when I had entered the gate. He also said that if I kept on the straight road until the end I should come to the Celestial City and be received with great rejoicing." Christian was delighted to tell his friend all that he knew about the journey in front of them. "Just think of it," he continued, "I shall have lost my burden; my sorrows will have turned to joy, and the Lord Jesus will comfort me for ever."

"I do hope He will receive me too!" replied his companion.

"Yes, indeed He will," said Christian, "if you are prepared to suffer for His sake and journey through difficult places."

Pliable was one who loved to enjoy the good things of life, and was not willing to work hard for them.

"I wonder what Christian means when he says we must be prepared to suffer and travel through rough places before we reach the Heavenly Land?" he mused. Turning to his companion he asked, "Do you suppose we shall have to overcome many obstacles in the Way?"

"Yes," replied Christian, "we shall have trials and temptations, but when we reach the Heavenly Shore we shall forget all our troubles and always be happy."

"Well, perhaps you are right. I will try not to think about the hard times ahead, and maybe they are not so bad as you imagine.''

Little did they known that trouble was to meet them in a very short while.

TWO

As they journeyed, the two friends were so interested in their conversation that they didn't notice a patch of marshland stretching before them. Up to this time they had found the road fairly easy and the ground firm under their feet; but now the way became more difficult.

"I should have thought that the Keeper of the Way would have kept the road in better repair," complained Pliable. "I do hope we come to firmer ground soon!"

"So do I," replied his friend. "Let us have patience and courage to keep going until we come to solid ground."

But the road became more treacherous. Puddles of mud and water faced them, and the presence of reeds proved that they were entering a swamp.

"Ouch! My feet are sinking in mud," cried Pliable.

"So are mine," replied his companion. They tried to reach hard ground, but they only found themselves farther in to the slough.

"If I can get out of this slimy marsh, I will turn back toward home. I was foolish to venture with you on this troublesome journey." Pliable began to complain bitterly.

"Is this the happiness you have promised me? If we are so unfortunate at our first setting out, what may we expect at our journey's end?"

"Do not be angry with me, good Pliable," pleaded Christian. "I never promised you that the Way would be easy. It is better to endure hardship in the Way than to go back to the City of Destruction. You must be brave and try to get out of this slough as soon as possible—but do not think of returning."

"Obstinate was right," replied the desperate man. "This way is beset by dangers and you must be very foolish if you still intend to continue the journey." At that moment he gained a solid piece of ground that was nearer to the City of Destruction and he quickly made his way back, saying, as he left Christian, "Good-bye, you silly man—I hope you will become sensible before it is too late."

"I cannot go back," replied the unhappy pilgrim, "for who will remove my burden from me in the city? Besides, I have promised Evangelist that I will not give up the struggle." The burden on his back made it very hard going for Christian and it caused him to sink deeper into the oozing mud. As he tried to raise one foot, the other went further in. He clutched hold of the reeds and pieces of broken rock, but they were not of much use. Thus he floundered about, hardly making an inch of progress. "If only someone would help me to get out of this horrid slough," he sighed, "but there appears to be no one in sight."

In the Book that he carried there was the story of a man who was placed into a horrible pit, at the bottom of which there were mud and lime. He was a very old man, and although he tried to climb out of his prison, his feet remained fast in the mire. There he languished for a long time, until a friend who had heard of the old man's terrible plight came to the head of the pit and lowered a rope so that the prisoner could be drawn out.

Christian knew this story, and he began to pray to God, asking Him to send a rescuer who would save him from the awful slough.

"If I had been more careful and looked to my path I would have seen this marshy ground, and thus have been able to walk at the side of it. I should have prayed before this, for no one but God can help me."

He was very ashamed that he had failed to pray before, but we always prefer to help ourselves when in trouble. It is not until we realize our helpless condition that we consent to cry to God for His aid. There appeared to be no response to Christian's prayer, and in great distress he cried out loudly, "Oh, Lord, save me, for I sink in deep mire where there is no standing."

"I am here to save you." Who was that calling from the brink of the slough? Christian raised his eyes toward the place where he heard the voice. A man was standing on a rock with a long piece of rope, ready to throw it in his direction. Christian struggled forward until he came within reach of the line, and caught hold of it as it was thrown to him. The kind stranger tugged at the rope, and after much heaving he managed to pull the sinking man to safety. Imagine the joy that came to Christian as he felt his feet on firm ground once more!

"My name is Help," said the man, "and it is my duty to

27

rescue pilgrims who get into the Slough of Despond.''

"Thank you for saving me from such a terrible plight," replied Christian. "It is so good of you to spend your time in this way."

"I do it because I love Jesus," said Help. "He has done so much for me."

The kind stranger went on to tell Christian more about his wonderful Master, and how he had been rescued from a worse plight than the Slough by the King of the Way.

"I am very puzzled about one thing," said the pilgrim. "How did you happen to be on the rock when I prayed for help?"

"Oh, I can explain that quite simply," replied the rescuer. "The Master prepared me for this work some long while ago; whenever a poor pilgrim cries in distress from the Slough, I am immediately commisioned to be there, ready to save. You should know that the Bible says 'Before they call, I will answer; and while they are yet speaking, I will hear.' ''

"Thank you so much for telling me about yourself and your work. I suppose you have made some thrilling rescues in your time? But tell me, why is this Slough of Despond so very treacherous? One would have thought that the King would instruct His servants to repair the ground."

"Ah," replied Help. "It is not possible to clear this Slough. Every pilgrim who makes up his mind to walk this way finds when the going is rough that he begins to despair, and I am afraid that the Slough is made deeper by reason of his wretchedness. True, there are a number of firm stepping stones placed through the middle of the marsh; but pilgrims are often so taken up with their troubles that they fail to see them.

"When you arrive at the lodge-gate you will find the path much firmer, and I know of no other Slough on the road."

"Good-bye, kind Help!" Christian held out his hand. "I shall always remember you and thank God for His kindness in sending you to me."

"Farewell, my dear friend. Always look to the path, for there is a way that seems right to a man, but the end of it is certain destruction. The road to the Celestial City is a straight and narrow one, and if you keep this in mind there will be no danger of wandering."

Thus Help took his leave of Christian, and remained near the Slough so that he could be of assistance to others who found themselves in the mire.

What had become of friend Pliable? You will remember that earlier he had gained a piece of firm ground, nearer to the City of Destruction. He quickly returned to his home and brushed the dirt from his clothes, saying to his surprised friends, "I am sorry that I was foolish enough to venture on pilgrimage with Christian; but fortunately I saw sense at last and have turned back. The Slough of Despond was a terrible experience, and I am not prepared to suffer any more hardships."

Some of his friends, including Obstinate, chided him, saying, "Why did you not listen to sound advice in the first place? If you had refused to believe Christian, you would not have experienced the horrors of that terrible Slough. Pliable is your name and pliable you are by nature. You are ready to believe any foolish person who tells you a cock-and-bull story. Take warning by this adventure and never attempt such a journey again.''

So Pliable remained in the city and was never seen in the Way any more.

Many other would-be pilgrims have started the journey like Pliable, and when trouble has overtaken them they have given up, returning to the place from which they came. Some have managed to dodge the Slough, only to flounder farther on in the Way.

There were many good things to be found in the City of Destruction, and most people who lived there were quite content to enjoy them. It was the knowledge that there was a City of Great Beauty far removed from theirs that caused many people to be discontented and to desire that Better Country. Christian was one of these sensible people and he did the right thing in starting on the Heavenly Way.

THREE

Having said farewell to his kind rescuer, Christian continued on his way, ever keeping the lodge-gate in view. He was looking very untidy, for his clothes were spattered with mud and badly torn; he had no stockings, and his shoes had fallen into the Slough. Poor man! If in the first few miles of his pilgrimage he met with such trials and difficulties, what could he expect farther on along the road?

"Come what may, I am determined to press forward," said Christian to himself. "Oh, my heavy burden! When will it be lifted from me?"

As he thus mused with himself a very fine-looking man came toward him, dressed in the height of fashion and wearing a large feather in his hat.

"How do you do, my poor friend," greeted the gentleman, who was known to most people in those parts as Mr. Worldly-wiseman. "You are in a mess. I see that you are covered with the slime of the Slough of Despond."

"Yes, unfortunately," replied Christian. "I accidentally fell into it some time ago and nearly perished."

"Why are you carrying that ugly bundle on your back?"

inquired the gaily-dressed gentleman.

"Oh, it is my awful burden of sin which I hope to lose when I am beyond the lodge-gate. I met a very kind gentleman who was exceedingly sorry to see my unhappy plight and directed me to the gate, where I should receive instructions and be told how to get rid of my burden."

Thus Christian told Mr. Worldly-wiseman all that had happened to him on the road.

"Was the man's name Evangelist?" asked the stranger.

"Yes, that was his name," replied the pilgrim, "and he told me that there was no other way in which I could find relief from my sins."

"Evangelist was wrong. I can tell you of a better way, that is less tiresome," said Worldly-wiseman.

If Christian had looked more closely at the stranger he would have discovered an arrogant expression in his eyes. He was a "know-all" and had no time for those who believed the message of the Evangelist. To him the only correct way to begin the journey toward the Celestial City was by ignoring the advice of the King's servants and to try finding the path by means of a long and difficult route.

It was a strange thing that many people preferred to go their own way instead of the narrow road advised by Evangelist. The message was simple: "Make your way to the lodge-gate and you will receive all the necessary instructions for the journey."

Worldly-wiseman continued his conversation thus: "There are so many dangers in the road that you are traveling and you will be very sorry when you come up against them. Be sensible and listen to my advice. I have a

Mr. Worldly-wiseman.

friend who is called Legality, a very clever fellow, skilled in the art of removing burdens from people's backs. If you will climb yonder hill, you will find his house at the top. Should he not be at home, ask his son to remove it for you. The son's name is Civility, and he is very nearly as useful as his father.''

It was not kind of the proud man to suggest to Christian that he should carry his heavy load up a steep hill, but the pilgrim was ready to act on his word.

''It is most kind of you to give me such good advice, and although the hill looks difficult, I am ready to climb it if only that I may be rid of my burden.''

''There's a sensible fellow,'' replied Worldly-wiseman. ''I can assure you that many have found relief at the top of that hill. Mr. Legality is a very old man, and he will tell you what to do before your load is finally lifted from off your back. You have no doubt heard of the Ten Commandments! Well, don't be surprised if he recites them to you. It will be necessary for you to obey these Commandments and not to break one of them; but I am sure you will be able to do this.''

Mr. Worldly-wiseman concluded his conversation with Christian by saying, ''Farewell; I hope that when I see you again you will be looking more cheerful and free from that bundle. They are waiting for me in the city, so I must be off.''

Christian bade the gentleman farewell, thanking him for his help and interest. He started to climb the hill, and such was his longing to be free from his troubles that he made light of the difficult climb for the first mile or so. The road became steeper as he climbed and the summit towered above his head. It almost seemed as if the mount would fall on him, and stretches of the path were strewn with rocks.

"I do not seem to be getting any nearer to the top of this hill," he thought. "surely it was not as high when I started climbing?" He trudged on, however, hoping to reach the house of Legality before dusk.

"My load is getting heavier as I climb higher," he cried. "What shall I do?" His poor aching feet were causing him to stumble on the rocky path, and no one met him to give a helping hand.

"What was that?" A loud rumbling came from farther up the hill, and it caused Christian to cry out in fear and alarm. Flash! Flash! Terrifying forked lightning dazzled his eyes and his knees began to knock together. He stopped in the path and could move neither up nor down.

"How foolish it was of me to heed that man's advice! He has been untrue to me, for I can never get relief in this mountain. If only I had kept to the Straight and Narrow Way and obeyed the instructions given to me by Evangelist!"

The lightning flashes became more frequent, accompanied by deafening crashes of thunder. Christian had never known such a dreadful storm, and he tried to take cover beneath one of the large rocks that was near at hand. As he peered through the gloom, the path almost vanished from his sight and he lost his sense of direction. It seemed to him that whichever way he went would be dangerous and he was afraid that he would fall over a precipice and be dashed to pieces.

"I must ask God to forgive me for wandering from His Way." He therefore knelt down and prayed this prayer:

35

"Dear Lord, take pity on me, and please send one of your messengers to help me down the hill back to the right path."

His lips trembled as he spoke to his Maker because he knew that he had no claim on God's mercy. The Lord is always willing to forgive, however, and He answered the weary traveler almost immediately by sending Evangelist once more to his aid. You will remember that it was this messenger who was first sent to Christian in order to show him the way to the lodge-gate.

The pilgrim arose from his knees and thought that he heard footsteps coming toward him. He heard a voice, but he could not understand what it was saying. Very soon, however, the messenger came within sight, and cried, "Why have you left the Narrow Way?" Christian looked toward the west and saw Evangelist hastening toward him.

"I'm so sorry," answered Christian, telling the good man of his talk with Mr. Worldly-wiseman.

"You can never hope to get free from your troubles by going to see Legality," advised Evangelist. "The Bible tells us that no one has ever been eased of the burden of sin by trying to keep the Law. It is true that the Ten Commandments are good and true, but the only One who has been able to satisfy God's Law is King Jesus. He is the One who governs the Celestial City, and one day you will see Him when you come to the end of your pilgrimage.

"Mr. Worldly-wiseman has been very wicked in three different ways. Firstly, because he advised you to turn aside from the Way; secondly, because he said that it was unnecessary for you to visit the lodge-gate; and thirdly, because he nearly brought about your destruction by telling you to climb this hill."

Christian was delighted to see Evangelist again, but he felt ashamed of himself for being so easily turned aside.

As it was getting very late in the afternoon, Evangelist advised the pilgrim to bestir himself. "You cannot stay here all night, for you will be exposed to the many storms that suddenly break on this mountain. Let me show you the way back to the Narrow Road." He led him by the hand until they came to the place where Christian had turned aside. "Yonder is the lodge-gate. Try not to wander any more." Evangelist left Christian with these words and the weary traveler trudged onward, hoping to reach the lodge-gate before nightfall.

The sun had begun to sink in the west when Christian came up to the gate, and knocked rather loudly for admittance.

Presently the noise of turning keys was heard, a gentleman opened the gate, and Christian had the joy of entering through the door into a flower-bordered path that led up to a stately mansion.

"My name is Goodwill, and I would like to see the scroll you have in your hand," said the gentleman.

Christian showed him his parchment and was asked to follow Goodwill, who led him up to the Interpreter's house.

After waiting for a few moments the door was opened by the owner and Christian was received with joy. He was shown into a lovely room that was very tastefully furnished, and here he was allowed to rest his weary feet until supper time. Before starting his meal he was able to have dressed the many wounds that he had received in the mountain when he had stumbled on the sharp rocks. He was thus made more presentable before sitting at table. You can imagine his disheveled appearance when he had arrived at the Interpreter's house. His clothes were ragged before he left the City of Destruction, and since that time he had experienced the terrible Slough of Despond with its slimy mud that had soiled his body.

The lovely meal that was placed before him was soon finished, for he was very hungry and ate ravenously.

When supper was over, he was asked to give an account of his journey thus far. The Interpreter was very sorry to learn of his many sufferings, but comforted him with the news that he would soon be rid of his burden.

"Get to bed now, and you will hear more about your deliverance tomorrow."

Thus the kind man took him to a lovely bedroom, and very soon the pilgrim was fast asleep.

FOUR

The morning sun was shining brightly into Christian's bedroom so that its warmth soon caused him to wake up. It seemed as if he had reached heaven already, but as he rose from the bed he realized that his burden was still on his back. He remembered, however, that the kind Interpreter had promised that soon his load would be lifted. With this encouragement he went downstairs to breakfast.

What a lovely breakfast it was too! There were all manner of good foods for him to eat, and he had a very good meal. He could not remember when he had last enjoyed such wonderful food, for when he was in the City of Destruction he had no appetite at all.

The Interpreter promised to show Christian over the house after breakfast and the pilgrim looked forward to an interesting time. The house consisted of a large number of rooms, in each of which were to be seen strange scenes. There was a lesson to be learned from every room, and the host undertook to explain the riddles to our friend.

In the first room Christian was shown a beautiful picture of a venerable old man. His eyes were gazing into Heaven and the best of all books was in his hand. His lips appeared to be speaking, and although the words could not be heard, the pilgrim understood that they were words of truth. The World (which appeared to be like the City of Destruction) was behind his back and a Crown of gold hung over his head.

"What does this picture mean, good Interpreter?" asked Christian.

"The aged man, whose portrait you see, is none other than the Apostle Paul, and the message of the picture is this:

"You will first notice that Paul is gazing into Heaven, and he does so because he has seen the King of that fair country and longs to be with Him. The Book in his hand is the Bible and he loved it very much. Some of the letters that he wrote are to be found within its pages. When Paul spoke, his words were true, and all those who heard him were affected by the message of his lips.

"You see that the World is behind his back, and that was true, for he left all earthly comforts that he might be a servant of the King.

"The Crown placed over his head was given to him at the end of his life by his Master as a reward for all his labors."

The pilgrim was very pleased to receive the answer to the riddle of the picture, and he supposed that St. Paul was one of the first pilgrims who traveled the difficult way to the Celestial City. The Interpreter agreed that this was so and he advised Christian to follow in the footsteps of the great Apostle.

In another room the pilgrim saw two children, whose names were Passion and Patience. Passion seemed very discontented, until someone gave him a bag full of costly treasures. He laughed at Patience and called him foolish for not asking for a similar gift. But Patience replied that he was quite content to wait until the Master was ready to give him of His bounty in His good time.

A short while after, Passion had spent all his money and began to be in want. His clothes became very ragged, and he was utterly wretched. At this time, Patience received of the Master a more precious gift, which he enjoyed for ever. Thus, he who laughed last, laughed best. Christian asked the Interpreter to explain the riddle to him.

"There are those people in life who are not content to await God's good time before they receive His benefits, but would enjoy themselves here and now. They are like Passion and soon find that the pleasures of this world are not abiding. Then they are indeed miserable and have no promise of future blessing. In contrast, there are those who are prepared to wait for God's blessing, knowing that He has promised Heaven to all who put their trust in Him." Thus the Interpreter explained this scene to the pilgrim.

"I understand this scene very well," exclaimed Christian. "There are a good many people like Passion in the City of Destruction. They are willing to risk their real happiness for the sake of a few passing pleasures, and they mock people like myself who are prepared to let go the riches of the city and start the pilgrim journey to the Celestial Land.

"Are there more rooms to see?" he continued.

"Yes, there are," replied the good man of the house, "and I want you to take special note of the room at the end of the passage."

As Christian entered, his eyes opened wide. There was a

large fire burning in the grate and an evil-looking man with a scowl on his face was throwing buckets of water into it. Of course the fire would be put out! But no—instead of this happening, the flames burned more brightly.

"What is the meaning of this?" asked Christian. "Why isn't the fire put out?"

"If you will look behind the grate you will see a wonderful person pouring oil into the flames, causing them to blaze in spite of the water," explained the Interpreter. "The good man is like the King of the Celestial City who will not allow the Evil One to extinguish the fire."

"This is indeed a riddle!" exclaimed the puzzled pilgrim. "Do tell me the answer."

The Interpreter thought for a moment. "How can I best explain this difficult scene?

"When pilgrims start their journey to the Heavenly City they are full of courage and seem 'on fire' for their King; but soon they find that an evil one tries to damp their spirits and cause them to be sorry they ever ventured. The King of the Way soon changes all this and the pilgrims remain cheerful and happy."

Gradually, Christian was shown the whole of the house and he learned a great deal by inquiring into the mysteries of its many rooms.

During his stay at the house he was able to gain strength for the journey that lay ahead, and although his burden was heavy upon him, he knew that in a very short while it would be removed. This gave him courage and he became almost happy.

At last the time came for him to continue his journey and

The fire that burned brightly.

he was told to keep close to the Narrow Way, not turning to the right or left.

"When you have traveled a few miles you will come to a Cross standing by the side of the road," advised the Interpreter. "It is there that you will lose your heavy burden—forever. Good-bye, and may the Lord bless you," he added.

Christian warmly shook the hand of his kind friend and set out on his way—eager to reach the small hill where the Cross was standing. He tried to run toward it, but was hindered by the terrible weight of his load. Presently he came up to the place and gazed longingly at the rough wooden Cross. As he looked, it seemed that the King was hanging there with a look of love and pity for the poor burdened pilgrim.

"My load of sin is slipping from my shoulders!" cried Christian. "Oh, thank you, dear Master, for bearing the punishment instead of me; what joy to be free from my sin and to be able to walk upright once more."

As he stood with his eyes fixed on the Cross, three angels appeared and greeted him with the words, "Peace by unto you." The first angel then said, "Your sins be forgiven." The second messenger stripped the rags from Christian and clothed him with garments that were suited to his journey. He also put a good pair of shoes on the pilgrim's feet that would protect them from the sharp stones and rocks. Another angel presented Christian with a sealed scroll and told him to hand it in at the gate of the Celestial City. A mark was put on the pilgrim's forehead so that people would know that he belonged to the King.

Our hero was so happy that he leaped into the air and went on his way singing.

The road on which he traveled was at this place fenced on each side by a wall, and he had no difficulty in keeping to the right way. He was able to walk faster now that his burden was gone, and he therefore made good progress. If any friend who had known Christian in the City of Destruction had met him now he would scarcely have recognized him, for his face was completely changed. "I feel like a new man now," he said to himself.

No longer would people stare at his burden and make rude remarks about his ragged appearance. His new clothes were different from those usually worn by the citizens of "Destruction," for they were neat and well cut.

Men like Mr. Worldly-wiseman dressed in gaudy materials, and were delighted when people remarked, "What a fine fellow he is! Must be someone of importance to sport such a brilliant coat, and look at the huge feather in his hat."

The shoes worn by Christian were most comfortable and he very quickly felt the benefit of their thick soles. He had not worn shoes for a long time because the rough road and slimy Slough of Despond had made them useless.

The songs that he sang as he walked along were about his King and the Celestial City.

The path sloped downward toward a pleasant valley, and on the farther side a very steep and difficult hill could be seen, over which the traveler was bound to go. As Christian reached the valley he noticed that three men were lying on some grass close to the Way. "What can be the matter with them?'' he thought. ''There appear to be iron chains fastened around their ankles.'' As he came up to the men he saw that they were asleep and it needed a great deal of shaking to awaken them.

''What is the matter?'' cried one as he shook himself, making his chains rattle.

''Why are you lying on the ground off the King's Highway?'' asked Christian. ''You are in great danger here and will fall a prey to any thief or wild beast that passes this way.''

The men had peculiar names—Simple, Sloth, and Presumption—and they answered the pilgrim in turn:

''I see no danger,'' said Simple. ''Yet a little more sleep,'' yawned Sloth. ''Every barrel must stand upon its own bottom,'' added Presumption.

At this, they rolled over and were soon fast asleep.

Christian tried to rouse them again, but they just grunted and then snored. The lesson Christian learned from these three foolish men was that a pilgrim should always be alert and ready to overcome every enemy. He should not be at the mercy of every evil one who would seek to injure him.

The chains on the ankles of the three men showed that they were bound by their own foolishness, slothfulness, and presumption. They had started their pilgrimage with high hopes and had no doubt come safely through the Slough of Despond; yet here they were, sleeping by the wayside— careless about their danger. We are not told what became of them, but it is believed that they never reached the Celestial City.

At last Christian could see that it was hopeless trying to

get them on their feet again. (He had offered to help them in the removing of their chains, but they had refused his aid.) Resuming his walk, he kept to the middle of the path and made good progress.

"I wonder what new adventures will be mine farther on along the road," he thought. "Whatever happens I am sure that the King will protect me, for He has promised to be with me unto the end."

There were many more adventures to come, but we must not anticipate them.

FIVE

"Who are those men tumbling over the wall?" wondered Christian as he continued his pilgrimage. Two men had just appeared from the other side and started to walk on the Narrow Way in front of him. Catching up to them, he asked them why they had climbed over the wall.

"We were born in the town of Vain-glory and are going to get praise in the Celestial City—it doesn't matter how we got into the Way, does it?" they asked.

"Yes, most certainly!" replied Christian. "You have not come by the way of the Cross, and I doubt whether you will be received into the Heavenly City."

"We're as good as you," retorted one of the men. "What does it matter if we did not come to the Cross?"

"It is not a question of your goodness," replied Christian. "I am not any better than you. Indeed, I have been very sinful, and until I came to the Cross a terrible burden was upon my back."

"Well, where is the difference then?" sneered the other. "We are on the same road with you, and that is all that matters."

"There is a difference," said the pilgrim. "I am the possessor of a sealed scroll that was given to me at the Cross and I was told to hand it in at the gate of the Celestial City. It is my passport to the mansions above. You have no scrolls and will therefore be refused admittance at the end of the road."

The names of the two men were Formalist and Hypocrisy—very difficult words that are not easily explained.

Formalist was a man who relied on outward show and thought that by this means he could enter Heaven. He was like the Pharisees mentioned in the Bible, who prayed long prayers and let everyone see how good they were. This man would go in for ceremony and the keeping of various laws. He would go without food for a long time and think that by so doing he would be sure of seeing the King in the Celestial City.

Hypocrisy was like his name—a hypocrite. That is, one who tried to make people believe him to be better than he really was.

Christian saw that it was no use talking with them, so he went ahead of them, and walked alone.

Having now got through the pleasant valley, the pilgrim noticed that the path began to ascend and he found that it was not so easy to get along. He was very thankful to have a good pair of shoes, for the road became rough and stony.

"Look at that steep hill ahead of us," cried Formalist. "Is there not some other way?"

"I certainly hope so," replied his companion, "but we shall soon know."

Christian did not speak to the two men and was determined to follow the road, wherever it led him. It appeared (from where he was walking) to go straight up the hill, so he mended his pace and strode forward.

"The fellow ahead of us is going to tackle the hill," observed Hypocrisy. "Silly man! Why doesn't he stop and try to find a better and more easy road?"

"Oh, he is far too stubborn," replied his companion, "but let us not concern ourselves with him."

As they drew nearer to the foot of the hill, two by-roads branched from the Narrow Way, the one winding to the left and the other to the right.

"These roads are what we have been looking for; which way will you take, Formalist?"

"I will walk to the left because it leads through some very pleasant country where I can enjoy myself. It will lead into the Narrow Way the other side of the hill, I don't doubt."

"Very well," replied Hypocrisy. "Since you choose the left, then I will turn to the right road. Good-bye, my friend; we shall meet again."

Little did they know that these two by-paths were called Danger and Destruction. The one led Formalist into a dark wood, where he was utterly lost, and the other led Hypocrisy into a wide desert full of black mountains, where he stumbled and fell, never to rise any more.

Let us not forget the pilgrim! How was he faring? Coming to the foot of the Hill Difficulty, he stooped down and drank of a clear cool spring. The water was very refreshing and he received added strength to mount the precipitous path, singing as he climbed:

"The hill, though high, I must ascend,
The rocky ground must overcome.
Its trial and pain shall not offend,
The way leads o'er to my blest Home."

The message of this song reminded Christian of the home he had left in the City of Destruction. He thought of his dear wife and the children, and prayed that they might see the danger in time. God heard his prayer, for some years later the family commenced the Pilgrim Way—but that is another story.

"It is a blessing that my burden is gone from off my back," Christian thought. "When I tried to climb the Mountain of Law my load made the journey impossible."

Up and up went the pilgrim and it seemed that he would never reach the top. He was not making as much progress now, for his limbs were tiring and the steep rocks were very difficult to clamber over. In places he had to go on his hands and knees.

"If only the Way were smoother, it would be less difficult," he moaned. "I shall have to take heed in my climbing, for it would be terrible if I slipped down into one of these ravines." Had he fallen down, there would have been little hope of his gaining the path again.

This side of the hill was exposed to the full fury of the wind, and apart from the large boulders, there was little protection from its chilling blast. Few trees grew in these parts owing to the high altitude—the mountain rose several thousand feet above the ordinary level of the ground.

"I am getting so tired," complained Christian. "If only I

could find somewhere to rest awhile.''

As he spoke he saw a cluster of trees in the Way farther up the slope. When he reached the spot he found it to be an arbor, or resting place, and a comfortable seat had been made where the pilgrim could recline. He seated himself and began to read from the scroll that had been given to him by one of the angels at the Cross.

The words that he read were very comforting, and he learned the wonderful fact that the King of the Celestial City knew all about him and would take care of him until the end of the journey. Christian spent some time reading and taking pride in the beautiful clothes that had been so kindly given to him.

It is not unusual for those who have been toiling hard to take a rest, and the tendency is to fall asleep. The weary traveler began to feel very drowsy and he soon fell fast asleep. The scroll that had been in his hand slipped to the ground and rolled underneath the seat.

It was toward evening when he was awakened by someone who said to him, ''Go to the ant, thou sluggard; consider her ways and be wise.'' On hearing these words Christian started up quickly, and forgetting the scroll, made the difficult journey up the hill. As he drew near to the summit he was startled by two men who were running down with more speed than judgment. They appeared to be very frightened and kept looking back, expecting to be overtaken by an enemy.

The name of the one was Timorous, and that of the other, Mistrust.

''Why are you running away in the direction of the City of

Destruction?'' inquired Christian.

Timorous answered they were going to the Celestial City and had up till now been able to overcome the perils of the Way. ''However,'' he continued, ''we did not expect to find the road more difficult as we went farther along it.''

''Yes,'' said Mistrust, ''for there are two ferocious lions standing in the way and we are sure that if we had met them they would have torn us in pieces.''

''You make me very much afraid,'' said Christian, ''but where can I go to be safe? If I turn back with you there awaits me only the City of Destruction. In turning aside, my feet will slip and I shall fall over a precipice. I must go on—for the promise is that the King of the Way will protect me.''

At this the two frightened men ran down the hill and were never seen on the Pilgrim Road again.

''I will have to make haste if I am to reach the top,'' Christian exclaimed. ''As I go on I will read in my scroll for comfort and help.''

He felt in his pocket, but could not find the parchment. ''Where can it be?'' he thought. This new difficulty made him very unhappy. He could not remember where he had left it until he thought of the little arbor about halfway down the hill.

''I must have left it on the seat,'' the pilgrim sighed. ''That means going back for it, and the hour is late.'' He then realized his foolishness in falling asleep and asked God to forgive him.

The journey back to the seat was not easy, because of the bad surface of the path; but after a while Christian reached the arbor and to his great delight discovered the scroll underneath the seat. Hastily he picked it up, putting it into his inner pocket. He made a resolve that he would never be so stupid again. The scroll was too precious to lose and he would need it when he arrived at the end of the road.

"I do hope it keeps light until the Palace Beautiful is reached," he thought.

The weary traveler trudged his way up again and at last arrived at the brow of the Hill Difficulty, where he paused to look at the wonderful scenery.

Away in the distance he could see a lovely Mansion surrounded by stately trees, and as the sun began to set, it shed its brilliant rays so that the whole place was ablaze with glory.

SIX

The road narrowed into an avenue of trees, at the end of which stood a small lodge. As Christian approached this avenue he stopped suddenly and listened intently.

Grr-rr-ll! "What is that growling noise?" Grr-rr-ll! Grr-rr-ll!

Two fierce lions were crouching one on either side of the path, looking as though they were ready to spring at the traveler and tear him to pieces. Christian's knees began to knock together and his teeth chattered. His first thought was for his own safety and he very nearly turned back like the two before him.

"Oh, I cannot go back," he cried, "for I shall bring dishonor on my King."

Timidly he walked forward, keeping to the middle of the path, and he thought of Daniel, who had been cast into a den of lions. He remembered how God had stopped the lions' mouths and delivered His servant from their clutches.

"The King can do the same for me, if I put my trust in Him," Christian told himself.

Thus he gained confidence as he pressed forward, singing

this song:

> "Dare to be a Daniel,
> Dare to stand alone,
> Dare to have a purpose firm,
> And dare to make it known."

The evil beasts began to roar most dreadfully, and in the failing light Christian could see their fiery eyes.

"Do not be afraid of them!"

Who was that who thus cried? Christian looked ahead and saw a man standing by the gate of the lodge.

"They are chained, and as you keep to the middle of the road, cannot reach you."

The pilgrim hastened past the wild animals and at last met up with the gentleman, who said, "I am the Porter of the Palace Beautiful, and my name is Watchful. Come into the lodge, for you must be tired by your long walk."

Christian told the Porter of his past journey and the many adventures that he had experienced since first he started on his pilgrimage.

"What is your name?" asked the good man.

"My name is now Christian, but I used to be known as Graceless until I was awakened from my dangerous condition in the City of Destruction."

"Why have you arrived here so late in the evening?" inquired the Porter. "The sun has set and it is now dark."

"I would have been here sooner except that, wretched man that I am, I slept in the arbor on the hillside. Even then I would have been here earlier, if I had not lost the scroll that was given me at the Cross. This meant that I had to return to the resting place, where I found it underneath the seat.''

At this point the Porter rang a bell and it was answered by a beautiful lady whose name was Discretion.

''This man is on a journey from the City of Destruction to Mount Zion,'' the Porter told her, ''but being weary with his hard climb up the Hill Difficulty he requires a night's lodging and good food.''

Discretion had come from the Palace Beautiful, and after inquiring about the pilgrim's many experiences she ran back to the door and called to three of her sisters, who appeared on the threshold.

The names of the three ladies were Prudence, Piety, and Charity, and they invited Christian into the Mansion, saying, ''Come in, noble pilgrim; this house was built by the King for weary travelers such as you.''

He bowed his head and followed them into the lovely abode, where he was given a seat at the supper table.

Before the meal was ready the sisters asked him questions about himself, and thus they began:

''What made you discontented with your life in the City of Destruction?'' asked Piety.

''I began reading a wonderful Book that told me about myself and my terrible danger. As I read, a heavy burden grew upon my back and I tried in vain to remove it. Many of my friends called me mad and would mock me as I cried out in anguish.''

''How did you find the way to the straight and narrow road?'' Piety was eager to know all the details.

''As I wept, a kind-looking man spoke to me and directed

me to the lodge-gate, thus setting me on the right road.''

"But did you not visit the house of the Interpreter?"
asked Piety.

"Yes, indeed," replied Christian, "and I saw some
wonderful scenes that I will remember for a very long time.''

"Do tell us about the many things you saw," pleaded
Piety.

Christian mentioned the beautiful picture depicting the
Apostle Paul and also the two boys named Passion and
Patience. "When I saw Passion receive those lovely
presents, I felt very envious of him; but soon he had spent all
his wealth and became wretched. No longer did I want to be
like him, for Patience had now received far greater treasures
that could never pass away.

"The fire that burned more brightly, in spite of the
wicked man's water throwing, filled me with amazement,
until I saw that wonderful Man pouring in the oil from
behind.''

"Who do you think the good Man was?" questioned the
lady.

"Oh, there is no doubt in my mind as to who poured the
oil into the flames—it was the King of the Celestial City,"
replied Christian.

"Supper is ready!"

What a welcome announcement. Servants were bringing
dishes to the table and the food looked very appetizing.

The pilgrim, who had been feeling very hungry, soon
emptied his plate; but there was a great variety of dishes, and
by the time he had sampled them all he felt much better.

During the meal the ladies spoke to him about the

Celestial City and its wonderful King. They delighted their guest by describing some of the beautiful things that he would see when he arrived in that blessed Home.

After supper was over they went into another room and Christian was able to relax in a very comfortable chair. They conversed until late in the evening, when his head began to nod.

"You are tired and need some sleep," observed one of the ladies. "Let us show you to your room."

Christian followed the lady upstairs and was given a large room with a very comfortable bed. He knelt down and thanked God for all His kindness—remembering his family who had remained behind in the City of Destruction.

He climbed into bed and very soon fell fast asleep. The night was peaceful and nothing disturbed his rest until the glorious sun shone into his room the next morning. The pilgrim was awakened by the singing of birds and he felt so refreshed that he began to sing with them.

The song that soon filled the room with its sweetness was this:

"Why should Jesus care for me,
And give me such sweet rest?
I feel as though I'm next to Heaven,
Where soon I shall be blest."

The window was a very wide one and gave a lovely view of the surrounding countryside. Green fields, adorned with all kinds of beautiful flowers, spread over the landscape, looking like some exquisite Eastern carpet.

Sheep with their lambs were peacefully grazing and the whole scene reminded Christian of the goodness of God.

He remembered that comforting psalm written by King David:

"The Lord is my shepherd;
I shall not want.
He maketh me to lie down in green pastures:
He leadeth me beside the still waters."

SEVEN

The kind sisters were up early and Christian could hear them making preparations for the morning meal. He therefore hurried to be ready when they should call him. Presently a servant came upstairs, and knocking at his door, announced that breakfast was served. Christian went downstairs and was shown into a very delightful room where the ladies were waiting for him at the table.

"How did you enjoy your night's sleep?" asked Prudence kindly.

"Very well, thank you, and I am so refreshed that I feel able to continue my journey and meet the dangers with renewed heart."

"Oh, we do not want you to leave yet, for we have planned some interesting things for you to do before you set out again," replied Prudence. "There are the treasures of the house and the wonderful library to see," she added.

After breakfast the sisters escorted him to a lovely library that contained many rare and fascinating books. There were records of the history of the Mansion and accounts of the many kind deeds performed by the King of the Celestial City.

Christian began to read and became so engrossed that he forgot the passage of time. The sisters left him alone, for they did not want to interrupt his studies.

The books spoke of the mighty acts of the King in making this world. They told of His great love for mankind in providing for their every need. There was that sad story of His cruel death, when he was taken by wicked people and put upon a Cross. Christian remembered the time when he came up to the Cross on a hill and he understood more fully the reason why his burden rolled from off his back.

He began to weep as he thought of all the sorrow that the King had passed through when He hung upon that Cross of wood, but was overjoyed when he came to the account of the Resurrection.

Not only were there recorded the acts of the King, but Christian discovered that His servants had accomplished many things. There was the story of Gideon, who gained a thrilling victory over the King's enemies with only three hundred men.

The mighty host of the Midianities had pitched their tents in a valley and were making preparation to fight the King's subjects. Such was their strength that they had no doubt about the outcome of the battle. Israel would be put to flight and many people destroyed.

The King commanded Gideon to go against this terrible host, and he obeyed.

Many thousand soldiers rallied round the banner of Gideon, but the King said there were too many. "These men will boast that they have gained the victory if you allow so great a number to go to the battle," He told Gideon.

At last three hundred men were chosen and they conquered that mighty army in this way:

Each man was given a trumpet, an earthen jar, and a lighted torch. Gideon led them to the edge of the valley where the Midianities were sprawled on the ground like grasshoppers. It was nighttime, and under cover of darkness each man took up his position around the camp, awaiting the command of their captain.

They had concealed their lighted torches inside the jars and held the trumpets in their right hands. Suddenly the cry rang out, "Break your jars!" There was a deafening crash of breaking pots and the torches flared up, making a ghostly glare all round the camp. At the same time each man blew on his trumpet.

The frightened Midianites started up from their sleep and supposed that some evil spirits had come upon them. They began to strike out with their swords and kill one another. Thus Gideon and his three hundred men put to flight the vast armies of their enemies.

Christian also read of the exploits of three men who lived in a foreign land ruled by a wicked king.

This king made a golden image and commanded his subjects to worship it. Shadrach, Meshach, and Abednego would not obey the king's command, refusing to bow down to the image. When the king heard of their disobedience he threw them into a burning fiery furnace, made seven times hotter than usual.

Imagine his amazement when he saw that the three men were not destroyed. They could be seen walking in the midst of the flames and their own King (for they were strangers in the land) was there with them.

He commanded the servants to release them from the furnace, and when they stood before him he saw that their clothes were unscorched.

Christian remained in the library for most of the day, and there was no time left in which to show him the rest of the house. He therefore had a meal and then retired to rest.

The next day the ladies led him into the armory, where they showed him numerous weapons for the use of pilgrims as they walked the Narrow Way. There were swords, shields, helmets, breastplates, and shoes that would never wear out. All these implements were piled into several heaps and were sufficient to equip every pilgrim who visited the house.

Christian was also shown some of the instruments used by the King's servants in days gone by. For instance, there was Moses' rod with which he parted the Red Sea, thus allowing the Children of Israel to pass through without harm; the pots, trumpets, and torches used by Gideon and his three hundred men were all there, together with the sling and stone used by David to slay Goliath of Gath.

As Christian viewed these wonderful things his heart was filled with pride to think that his King could perform such wonderful deeds through ordinary pilgrims, without much strength of their own.

> "Shamgar had an oxgoad,
> David had a sling,
> Dorcas had a needle,
> Rahab had some string.

"Samson had a jawbone,
Moses had a rod,
Mary had some ointment
All were used for God."

Having spent some time in the armory Christian was asked if he would like to view the gardens and surrounding countryside.

"Yes, please. I thought the scene from my bedroom window was enchanting," he replied.

The sisters were delighted to show him the estate, and they wandered about the grounds with him, while he admired the beautiful flowers and trees.

"If you will come into the house we will take you to the top floor, where a better view can be had of that distant range of mountains." They were pointing in the direction of the Celestial City.

When the friends reached the highest room they opened the window and asked Christian to look out across the landscape.

"The mountains are quite clearly seen from this height," he exclaimed. "What are they?"

"These mountains are called Delectable, and the beautiful country around is called Emmanuel's Land," replied one of the sisters.

Christian was told that when he arrived at the borders of Emmanuel's Land he would be able to see the Celestial City, but only on a clear day. There were many shepherds wandering over the mountains, he was told, and they would be a great comfort to him.

"I really think that I must be starting my journey once more," he said, after gazing at the Delectable Mountains with great longing. "I would like to be there and experience the delights of that beautiful land."

"Very well—you shall start on your way as soon as we have fitted a suit of armor upon you," replied Discretion.

The sisters led the way downstairs into the armory and sorted out the equipment best suited to his needs.

He was clothed with the Helmet of Salvation, the Breastplate of Righteousness, the Shield of Faith, and shoes to enable him to walk the Pilgrim Way. In his hand they placed a sword—called the Sword of the Spirit.

"With this armor you will be able to overcome all the attacks of the enemy." Discretion encouraged him with these words.

The time had come for him to depart, and after saying farewell to his kind friends, he made his way to the gate and met the Porter who had so kindly introduced him to the ladies.

"Has any other pilgrim passed this way recently?" Christian asked.

The Porter replied that one called Faithful had just gone down the hill in the direction of the Celestial City, and if Christian made haste he would overtake him.

"Thank you, kind sir. I will take your advice and put my best foot forward."

Christian hurried down the path. Although he had expected the ladies to remain in the Palace Beautiful after he had bidden them farewell, he was pleased when they came after him and insisted on accompanying him as far as the

Valley of Humiliation.

This valley was met at the bottom of the hill, where the sisters gave Christian a loaf of bread, a bottle of wine, and a cluster of raisins.

"Take some of this food now," advised Discretion, "for you will need it—now that you have entered the valley."

They finally left him and returned to the Mansion, where preparations were being made for further guests.

EIGHT

If Christian had felt any pride in having such a beautiful suit of armor, this valley soon altered his feelings. He began to feel downcast and a little afraid.

Suddenly, he heard a noise of flapping wings. The pilgrim grasped his sword more firmly in his hand and covered himself with the shield. A terrible monster was coming toward him and Christian's first impulse was to run back to the Mansion.

The armor worn by Christian did not cover his back; this was left unprotected, so he had to face up to the monster and prepare for battle.

The name of the monster was Apollyon, and he was hideous, having scales like a fish, wings like a dragon, feet like a bear, and a mouth like that of a lion.

As he spoke there came from his nostrils fire and smoke, and the first words that he uttered were these: "Who are you? Where are you going, and from what city have you come?"

"My name is Christian," replied the frightened pilgrim, "and I come from the City of Destruction. My destination is

71

the Celestial City, and please do not hinder me from going there.''

''You are one of my subjects,'' cried the evil one, ''for I own the City of Destruction. Go back at once, or I will strike you down with my fiery darts.''

''I cannot go back and am no longer your subject,'' replied Christian. ''The King of the Celestial City has made me His servant and He is a far better Master. Your service was slavery and your wages insufficient to live on.''

''I will pay you better wages if you will consent to return to my domain,'' continued Apollyon. ''You can have all the riches of the earth.''

''It would be foolish for me to gain the whole world and lose my own soul. My King has promised me a home in Heaven and my reward will be a crown if I continue to serve Him faithfully.''

''You have already been unfaithful in your service for Him. Didn't you fall into the Slough of Despond?''

''That is true,'' replied the pilgrim a little shamefacedly, ''but my King has forgiven my sins and promised not to remember them any more.''

Apollyon was very angry when he heard the pilgrim's remarks and said, ''I am an enemy of this King. I hate Him, His Laws, and His People.''

He strode toward Christian and threw a flaming dart at his heart. This was where the Shield served our hero well, for he caught the missile so that it fell harmlessly to the earth.

Then the pilgrim lunged at the monster with his Sword, and Apollyon barely avoided it. He began to aim darts at Christian and they fell as thick as hail. Some wounded the

Christian overcomes Apollyon.

poor man in the head, hand, and foot, and he cried out to his King to save him from the power of the evil one. His prayer was heard, for he made such a strong thrust at the giant with his Sword that the monster reeled back and flew away.

When the battle was over, Christian gave thanks and said, "He has delivered me from the evil one. Blessed be His Name."

He continued on his way, much fatigued by reason of his gruelling fight, and there seemed to be no improvement in the valley. It was aptly called Humiliation and the sun hardly shone through the gloom. No longer could he see the beautiful landscape nor the Delectable Mountains.

Christian remained on his guard against any possible enemy and his Sword was drawn ready to strike. Although he was downcast he realized that the King was looking after him and he took comfort from this thought.

Just then he saw two men coming from a dark valley that was more terrifying than Humiliation.

"Go back if you value your life," they cried.

"Why, what is in yonder valley?" Christian asked of the two strangers.

"Terrible things. It is as dark as pitch and horrible creatures are there making noises like thunder."

"It is evident that the Narrow Road goes through the dreadful place," replied Christian, "so I will have to pluck up courage and make my way into it."

"If you are so foolish and will not listen to reason," the two men exclaimed, "we will leave you to your fate."

They then left Christian and were not seen in the Way again.

The pilgrim looked to his armor and saw that his Sword and Shield were before him. Thus he ventured into the darkness and stepped very carefully lest he should fall into a pit. Although he could not see, he managed to keep to the middle of the path, and it was as well that he did so, for on the left of it was a quagmire and to the right a wide ditch.

To add difficulty upon difficulty, the road narrowed and Christian was just able to place one foot before the other, making very slow progress.

When he reached the middle of the Dark Valley he saw, by reason of the lurid red flames, a horrible fiery pit, very much like a gigantic furnace. The narrow path was illumined by the glow and he quickened his pace so that the danger might be passed as soon as possible.

"What an awful place!" he groaned. "Thank you, dear King, for protecting me thus far, and give me the strength to reach the end of this dread valley."

As he prayed to God he received courage to continue along the Way, but there were more dangers to meet and he often felt like turning back.

Sometimes he imagined that evil ones were near him, and once he heard the roar of a ferocious lion. He grasped the Sword, ready for a possible attack, but nothing touched him as he groped along.

Gradually the valley became lighter, and to his great joy, he could see the end of it in the distance.

Each step brought him nearer to safety, and as he pressed forward the Way became easier. A snake slithered into a pit at the side of the path, an ugly lizard crouched in the crevice of a rock, and an owl hooted dolefully overhead.

"I am not afraid of you now," cried Christian, "for the end of this dismal place is not far away."

Just then the sun shed some of its glorious rays into the valley, lighting up the path before him. The pilgrim almost leaped for joy, but he still had to be careful—keeping in the middle of the Way.

He could now see the many pitfalls and the deep ditch that ran alongside the road. Had Christian fallen into one of these holes or slipped into the ditch, it would have been almost impossible to regain the path.

The Way began to rise a little, and as Christian reached the higher ground, he breathed more freely. He knelt down and thanked his King for preserving his life thus far.

As he arose from prayer a little song came to his lips:

"He has kept me from falling,
And will guide to the end.
What a wonderful Saviour!
What a wonderful Friend!"

A little farther up the road Christian saw another pilgrim, and on coming nearer saw that it was the man called Faithful. He had known him when they both lived in the City of Destruction.

Such was his haste to catch up with Faithful that he passed him before he could stop running. As he slowed down his foot caught in a rut and down he crashed to the ground. It was necessary for the other pilgrim to help him up again, and after brushing the dust from his armor, Christian thanked Faithful for his timely aid.

"We can walk together now and talk of the things that interest us both. When did you decide to venture on this pilgrimage?"

"It was some time after you, dear Christian," replied his friend. "The town was in an uproar when you fled from it with that heavy burden upon your back. Some told me of your warning that the whole place would soon be destroyed, and I believed you to be truthful."

"Did others agree to accompany you out of the city?" asked Christian.

'No, unfortunately," replied Faithful. "Although many were scared, they did not have the wisdom to leave their doomed homes."

"You found the lodge-gate, I suppose ?"

"Yes—that was the necessary start to my pilgrimage," replied Faithful. "Fortunately, I could plainly see the Slough of Despond, and I managed to escape it," he added.

They recounted to one another the thrilling adventures that had come their way, and in so doing the two friends passed many interesting hours.

Unnoticed, a man came up to the two pilgrims and walked at their side. Faithful, who had been engrossed in his conversation with Christian, turned his head and realized the presence of the stranger.

"Are you going to the Heavenly Country?" he asked.

"Yes, indeed," replied the man, whose name was Talkative.

"That is well. Can we have your good company?"

"I count it a privilege to walk with you, good pilgrims, and it will be jolly to talk to you as we journey along."

It was not long before the two friends became bored with the stranger's conversation. He was able to talk about everything, but his words were idle words. Christian very soon recognized Talkative and remembered him in the City of Destruction. He was a man who talked, talked, talked, but never did any good in his life.

Taking Faithful aside, Christian acquainted him with the truth about the talkative one, and it was not long before he showed himself in his true colors. It could be said of him that he was "all talk and no do."

A few yards farther on Talkative left Christian and Faithful, and the two friends continued their journey toward the Celestial City.

Presently, Faithful thought he heard footsteps behind them, and turning his head, saw Evangelist, who was trying to catch up to them.

"Look, Christian!" he exclaimed. "An old friend of ours is behind. Let us wait for him."

They were delighted to see him once more, and after exchanging greetings, Evangelist began to ask the pilgrims questions about their many adventures in the Way.

"I am glad to hear of your progress along this Narrow Road," he told them, when he had been acquainted with the facts. "You have been very brave and the King is most pleased with you."

"We have overcome our difficulties with His help and have thanked Him many times," replied Christian.

"I am glad that you have remembered to thank the King: so few people are willing to do that. Will you receive some advice from me?" asked Evangelist. "I want to warn you about the town that can be seen a little way ahead of us.''

"We are always ready to receive sound advice from you, dear friend," replied Faithful.

"Very well," continued the good man. "This town is very wicked and you will have to be on your guard against possible enemies. Some of the citizens will mock you, some will do you harm; but be of good courage, for the King is with you, although He cannot be seen."

NINE

Vanity Fair—what a strange name to give to a market town!

The kind of fairs that we are used to are places where people amuse themselves. There are the swings, merry-go-rounds, hoop-las, and sideshows. Bunting is draped around and the whole scene is one of merriment and laughter. Sometimes we are able to watch the circus, in which lovely white horses, ridden by daring riders, canter about, and clowns make us laugh with their acrobatic stunts.

From early days there have been fairs, and in England they have been held at Barnstaple, Widecombe, Mitcham, and Barnet, to name just a few towns.

At these old fairs people exchanged goods, farm produce, and livestock; there they met old friends and enjoyed harmless pleasures.

Vanity Fair was unlike any of these, for it catered for wicked people who committed all manner of crimes against one another.

The two pilgrims had now reached the outskirts of this town and saw that the Way went through the center of it.

They remembered the good advice given to them by Evangelist and continued their journey without stopping to examine some of the tents and buildings that were at the side of the path.

The citizens who thronged the town were amused at the strange appearance of the travelers. Christian excited the most interest, for his suit of armor was quite unlike anything that the townspeople had seen before.

Faithful's sober clothes caused the onlookers to laugh and make rude comments.

Many years before, the King of the Celestial City had passed through Vanity Fair and the chief lord of the town invited Him to buy some of the vanities that were for sale. Beelzebub escorted the King through the streets of the Fair, showing Him all the kingdoms of the world in a very little time, hoping by this means to bring discredit upon His Blessed Name. But the pleasures of the Wicked City held no attraction for the King and He spent not so much as a dime on the goods displayed.

Not only the strange clothes of the pilgrims caused amusement, but their speech was foreign to the men of the Fair. When they spoke to one another, their language was not understood. The speech of the pilgrims had altered since they had left the City of Destruction and their dialect was a heavenly one.

One of the stallholders mocked them as they passed and asked them if they would buy some of his wares. Christian replied in the same dialect, so that it would be possible for the man to understand. "We buy the Truth."

At this the people who were standing around began to

82

taunt the pilgrims and made as though they would strike them. The crowd grew so large that it attracted some of the officers, who reported the matter to their prince.

Beelzebub commanded that the two strangers be brought before a judge who would hear their case. Before this was done, however, Christian and Faithful were beaten and smeared with dirt. After these insults were heaped upon them they were put into an iron cage where everyone could mock and ill-treat them.

A few of those who stood around were sorry to see the terrible plight of the poor pilgrims and they began to quarrel with the ruffians, telling them to leave the strangers alone.

Very soon a large angry crowd had gathered outside the cage and the people took sides. Some favored the poor prisoners and the others were against them; thus a brawl developed and many were hurt in the fighting. The noise of battle soon brought the policemen on the scene, and they had to use their weapons in order to break up the rioters.

Christian and Faithful were accused of causing this riot, so they were taken from the cage and grievously beaten with cruel whips. With their backs sore and bleeding they were again locked up in the prison, and there they remained for many days. Heavy chains were placed around their bodies and their feet were made fast in the stocks.

The men of the Fair arranged a trial for the pilgrims, and on a certain day they were taken to the courthouse and placed inside the dock.

The judge, whose name was Lord Hate-good, was an evil-looking man and seemed very fierce in his long white wig.

Three people had been engaged to bear false witness against Christian and Faithful.

The first witness, whose name was Envy, told the judge that Faithful was a wicked man who spoke against the Fair and incited the people to rebellion. It seemed that Faithful was the one chosen for the most abuse, and each of the three witnesses testified against him.

The names of the other two were Pickthank and Superstition.

Pickthank informed the judge that Faithful had insulted their Prince Beelzebub and stated that his King would finally destroy him. "He also spoke against our nobility, including the Lord Old-man, the Lord Carnal-delight, the Lord Desire-of-vain-glory, the Lord Lechery, and Sir Having Greedy," Pickthank concluded.

When Pickthank had finished speaking the judge addressed Faithful with these words:

"You are a traitor and deserve to be condemned to death, but first I will give you a chance to reply to the accusations made against you by my honest witnesses."

"Very well, Judge," replied Faithful. "I will endeavor to speak for myself, and, most of all, for my King.

"Remarks that I made to the people of your town were not intended to insult anyone who was honest and good living. I merely said that the laws and customs opposed to the Bible were wrong and that they should not be obeyed. It is true that I spoke against your prince, who should be cast into the pit with all his followers. The King of the Celestial City will one day bring him to justice."

At this, the judge turned to the jury and said that it was

quite evident that Faithful was guilty, but it was their duty to say whether he was to die or be released.

The jury retired from the court to consider their verdict, but it did not take them very long to come to a decision.

What a motley crowd they were, and their names gave them away:

Mr. Blind-man, Mr. No-good, Mr. Malice, Mr. Heady, Mr. High-mind, Mr. Enmity, Mr. Liar, Mr. Cruelty, Mr. Hate-light, Mr. Implacable, and two others.

Soon they filed back into court, and the foreman pronounced the verdict. "Guilty!" he cried.

Lord Hate-good agreed with them and he therefore sentenced poor Faithful to death. Thus this gentle pilgrim became a martyr, and received an abundant entrance into the Celestial City, where he dwells forevermore. Christian was present when Faithful died, and he was encouraged as he looked into the sky, where a chariot and horses could be seen awaiting the arrival of his friend. He had not received the same sentence, but was put back into prison, where he remained for a long time.

It may be interesting to describe Vanity Fair in more detail.

First, it was ruled over by Prince Beelzebub, and spread right across the Way to the Celestial City.

It was not possible for any pilgrim to make the journey to the Heavenly Land without passing through the Fair. The town was divided into streets and rows called by such names as American Row, Britain Row, French Row, Italian Row, Spanish Row, German Row—the countries of the earth were all to be found there. The history of the place went back some 6,000 years, and during that long time many dark deeds had been committed. Without question, the darkest of them all was that done on a hill called Calvary.

The King had not forgotten the poor pilgrim in prison and Christian was comforted with the knowledge that he was not alone. Although he could not see his Saviour, he felt His Presence.

Christian would often pray for deliverance, and at last the opportunity came when he was able to escape from the prison. We are not told how it happened. Perhaps the guard grew careless and left the gate unlocked.

There were once two men who were very faithful to their King, so much so that the wicked men of their day put them both into prison. Instead of bemoaning their fate they sang praises to God, and the prison walls echoed with the sound of their voices. Suddenly, while they were yet singing, there was a mighty earthquake, and their chains fell off. The prison doors flew open and they were free to escape; but, instead, they remained where they were. Imagine the consternation of the jailer when he realized the situation!

If any of the prisoners had escaped he would have been severely punished. He began to be sorry for his sins (he had been a cruel man), and, trembling, he came into the cell where the two men were. He asked them how he could be forgiven, for he knew that they were God's messengers. Paul and Silas were able to point him to Jesus, who alone was able to forgive sins.

What a change came over the jailer! Instead of being cruel he became gentle and kind, binding up the wounds of the men and bringing refreshment for them.

It may have been by means of an earthquake that Christian found himself free. We are not told—we can only guess. Suffice it to say that once again he was seen to be making his way toward the Celestial Road.

TEN

Christian quickly found his way out of Vanity Fair, and feeling sad, sang a hymn in memory of Faithful, who had so bravely given his life for his King.

Christian was now alone, and this fact made him very unhappy.

"If only someone would journey with me on the Pilgrim Way I should be so pleased and the time would pass more pleasantly," he thought.

As he reached a turn in the road, a stranger met him and greeted him in the following manner:

"Good morning, sir! Will you allow me to accompany you on your pilgrimage? I was so impressed by your behavior in the Fair that I purposed becoming a pilgrim, and your King has accepted me."

"What is your name?" asked Christian.

"My name is Hopeful, and I became so when I learned about the Celestial City from the lips of Faithful and your good self."

"This is an answer to my prayer," exclaimed the lonely pilgrim. "I shall be delighted to have your company on the difficult journey that lies ahead."

The two new friends went forward arm in arm, and all the unhappiness of Christian went from him as they conversed about the things that interested them most.

"Tell me about your adventures since first you started on your pilgrimage," said Hopeful.

"There is much to tell," replied Christian, "but I love to recall all the wonderful things that have happened to me in the Way. The difficulties were many and the trials hard to bear; but in all these I have been more than a conqueror through Him who loved me so."

Hopeful was so enthralled by the stories that he failed to notice a gentleman who walked ahead of them.

"Who is the traveler along the road?" asked Christian. "Let us catch up to him and inquire."

This gentleman, who had attracted the interest of the pilgrim, was a very fine-looking man. His clothes were of the best materials and his manner grand.

"Where are you going, stranger?" asked Hopeful.

"I am making my way to the Celestial City and my home town is the beautiful City of Fair-speech."

"I have heard of this place," replied Christian. "Is it not a wealthy town?"

"Yes, I can assure you of that, and I have many rich relatives there. You will perhaps know some of them. There are my Lord Turn-about, my Lord Time-server, my Lord Fair-speech, from whose ancestors the town first received its name; also Mr. Smooth-man, Mr. Facing-both-ways, Mr. Any-thing, and the minister of our parish, Mr. Two-tongues. He was my mother's brother, and to tell you the truth, I am become a gentleman of good quality; yet my great-grandfather was but a waterman, looking one way and rowing the other.''

''Are you a married man?'' asked Christian.

''Yes indeed, and my wife is the daughter of a grand lady whose name was Lady Feigning. She has come of a very honorable family and is so gentle of birth that everyone who knows her treats her with respect. Our family differs from those who are strict in their religion; but only in two small details. First, we never strive against wind and tide; secondly, we love religion when everything is easy and pleasant.''

Christian stepped aside to speak to Hopeful alone. ''This gentleman is none other than By-ends, of Fair-speech, and he is a cunning fellow who would make us believe him to be honest and good.''

Turning to the stranger he said, ''Are you not By-ends?''

''That is not my name, but it is a nickname that is given me by my enemies. However, I must be content to bear this name as a reproach. Other men have borne the sneering of their fellows, so why shouldn't I?''

''Have you not deserved this name?'' asked Christian.

''Never!'' replied the stranger. ''The worst thing I do to give people an occasion to so nickname me is that I always jump on the right side of the fence and agree with anyone, if by so doing I can make some money.''

''I am afraid that your name suits you,'' exclaimed Christian, ''and I do not think that you will want our company for long. If you walk with us you will have to go against wind and rain, and have religion when the Way gets difficult and rough.''

At this the gentleman began to lag behind, and the pilgrims continued their interrupted conversation.

By-ends was soon joined by three other men whose names were Mr. Hold-the-world, Mr. Money-love, and Mr. Save-all. By-ends knew these gentlemen, for he had been to school with them in his boyhood days. The teacher of that school was one Mr. Gripeman, and it was situated in a market town called Love-gain in the county of Coveting. The schoolmaster did not teach ordinary subjects, but instructed the boys in the art of getting riches by any means.

By-ends was asked by his friends about the two pilgrims walking ahead of them.

''They are a couple of men who are going on a pilgrimage to the Celestial City.''

''Why did they not walk with you?'' inquired Money-love.

''Because they are too strict and do not tolerate my ideas about religion. They told me that, although the Way became difficult, yet would they continue on the road.''

''That is silly,'' exclaimed Hold-the-world. ''I do not mind the journey while the going is good, but should it become difficult I will make for some place of ease—off the road.''

''So will I,'' agreed Save-all. ''He is a fool who will risk his comfort for the sake of the pilgrimage.''

''As we are agreed on all these questions,'' said By-ends, ''will you allow me to ask your advice on a certain matter? Suppose a minister desires to increase his living and obtain a larger church, would it be honest for him to change some of his views and preach to please his new congregation?"

"Certainly," replied Money-love. "For many reasons—namely:

"(1) It is good to desire a larger church so that he can preach to more people.

"(2) There would be a greater need to study and preach more sermons.

"(3) To please his people is very good, even if it means denying some of the truths of the Bible.

"(4) The fact that he gets more money is a blessing that should not be despised."

Thus they reasoned with one another and, quickening their steps, they caught up with Christian and Hopeful.

"What do you think of my question?" asked By-ends of the two pilgrims. He had acquainted them with the conversation, and Christian replied:

"Even a child would see the folly of the answer given by Money-love: people have tried to use religion for their own gain in the past. Do you not remember the story of Judas, who appeared to be as good as the other disciples, and yet followed Jesus because he held the purse? He finally sold his Master to the enemy for thirty pieces of silver."

By-ends and his three friends did not like Christian's answer, so they fell back again and allowed Christian and Hopeful to continue their journey alone.

The two pilgrims were now passing through a pleasant plain called Ease, which they found very restful, for they had become a little tired by the Way.

At the far side of the plain there was a silver mine, and a gentleman named Demas was beckoning the pilgrims to come and see. The mine was a little off the road and Christian became suspicious of the stranger.

"Do not be persuaded to go over," he advised Hopeful.

"Do come over and see the wonderful mine," pleaded Demas. "If you dig deep enough you will discover riches untold, and be able to live like gentlemen until the end of your days."

"We do not want the riches of the mine," replied Hopeful, "for we are promised far greater wealth when we reach the Celestial City."

"Very well; if you are so foolish as to refuse this silver, there is nothing more to be said." Thus Demas turned away from them and sought to persuade others to dig in the mine.

Soon the four men who were following the pilgrims reached the spot, and Demas was successful in getting them to descend. By-ends and his companions were never seen in the Way again, for they were content to search for treasure.

"There seems to be a monument standing on the side of the road," exclaimed Christian. "Let us read the inscription."

"Remember Lot's Wife."

These were the words at the base of the figure, and Christian remembered the story of the destruction of Sodom. Lot, who lived with his family in the city of Sodom, received a message that he was to flee away, because God was going to destroy the town with fire. The people had been very wicked, and despite many warnings they were unrepentant.

Two angels appeared to Lot and gave him instructions concerning his journey. "If anyone turns to look back at the city, that one will be changed into a pillar of salt," the angels

Demas beckoning the pilgrims to go down the silver mine.

warned.

At last a small company comprising Lot, his wife, and his two daughters fled from Sodom, and then God caused fire to burn the entire place. Mrs. Lot was very unhappy at having to leave her home, for she loved her neighbors and did not mind their wickedness. As they hurried away she turned her face to see the terrible sight of the burning city, and was immediately turned into a pillar of salt.

Thus she remained, as a warning to others; and people learned that it is a sin to turn back from the task that God has set them.

"Let us take notice of this warning and press on toward the Heavenly City," exclaimed Hopeful.

ELEVEN

After leaving the monument the pilgrims quickened their pace, ever remembering the lesson of the pillar of salt. Although the plain called Ease had been pleasant, yet it lacked the lovely green hedges and trees that had abounded in other parts of the Way.

They had now reached a river that flowed alongside the road, and as they were very thirsty, the two friends stooped down by the river and drank of its pure waters.

This river was called by two names: first, "The River of God," so named by King David in one of his beautiful psalms. St. John called it "The River of the Water of Life."

The trees that had been absent in the plain could be seen growing on the banks of the stream, and Christian ate some of the leaves. He found that his aches and pains vanished away and therefore advised Hopeful to eat some of the leaves also.

A beautiful meadow stretched out before them on either side of the river, and flowers of every hue grew in abundance.

"Let us lie down on the grass and rest," said Hopeful.

"A very good suggestion," replied his friend, who made himself comfortable and was soon fast asleep.

Hopeful did not lose much time in following the example of the sleeper, and there the two pilgrims remained until the warm sun gently awakened them the next morning.

Feeling hungry, they gathered the delicious fruits of the trees and drank of the crystal waters.

They were reminded once again of that most beautiful psalm:

"The Lord is my shepherd;
I shall not want.
He maketh me to lie down in green pastures:
He leadeth me beside the still waters."

Christian and Hopeful spent many days and nights here and they were both fully restored in soul and body.

The time came, however, for them to continue their journey; and with much regret they left the River of God with its lovely surroundings.

The road became rocky as they went forward and their feet were hurt on the rough stones. The pilgrims soon forgot the pleasant times spent by the river and began to complain about the hardness of the Way.

But soon they reached a soft, grassy meadow that stretched away from the road and was entered by a stile.

"Let us turn aside and walk in the field—we can make sure that we follow the road," exclaimed Christian. "The path will be easier for our feet."

They clambered over the stile and proceeded to walk the

other side of the hedge, ever keeping the main road in view One thing they forgot, however: the evening closed in upon them and very soon it was quite dark.

It was now impossible to see the road, and they wandered helplessly until, exhausted, they fell upon the grass and went fast asleep.

They had tried to find their way back to the stile, but the ground was so treacherous and so many deep ditches full of water were everywhere that they had been unable to find the stile again.

The pilgrims slept uneasily until the morning, and you can imagine their horror when an ugly giant rudely awakened them with the words:

"Why are you trespassing on my grounds, you good-for-nothing fellows?"

"Oh, sir," pleaded Christian, "we were journeying to the Celestial City and, seeing your meadow, turned aside to walk on the soft grass."

"How dare you trample on my meadow! Do you not know that I can destroy you for being so venturesome?"

The giant growled and prodded them with his huge boot. "Get up at once and come along with me."

The two pilgrims were so terrified that they obeyed him without question, and he drove them into a dark, forbidding castle. The name of this castle was Doubting, and the giant who owned it Despair.

When the heavy iron door shut against them the terrible giant pushed the pilgrims into a dark and dismal dungeon, where they remained from the Wednesday morning until Saturday night—without food or drink.

Giant Despair had a wife whose name was Diffidence, and she was as ugly as her husband. When the loathsome creature reached his own apartments he told his wife all about the unhappy pilgrims.

"What shall we do with them?" he asked her.

She advised him to beat them without mercy in the morning.

He therefore arose early and made his way to the dungeon. Under his arm he carried a rough cudgel and around his waist hung a bunch of rusty keys. Arriving at the door of the prison, he opened it with one of the keys, and seeing the two poor men lying there, he began to beat them with the cudgel.

"Oh, do spare us!" they cried in their anguish. "We will not trespass on your land again."

"I am not going to let you out of my castle," replied Despair. "You will remain here until you die."

Every morning he visited them, and their lives were so miserable that they almost wished themselves dead.

"Are the pilgrims still alive?" Diffidence asked the giant some days later.

"Yes indeed—they appear to be sturdy rogues and do not die easily."

"Well, listen to me," continued the woman. "When you visit them tomorrow take them into the castle yard and show them the skulls and bones of the other pilgrims who have died at our hands."

When the morning came the giant obeyed his wife and drove the helpless men out of the dungeon into the yard to see the horrible remains of past pilgrims who had found themselves in the clutches of that evil man.

Christian and Hopeful escaping from Doubting Castle.

"You will be like these in ten days' time," he threatened. At this he beat them again and pursued the pilgrims back to the dungeon.

They lay all that day in a terrible plight, and when the evening came Christian began to think of escaping. Suddenly he remembered a key tucked away in his breast pocket.

"What a silly man I am to be sure!" he cried. "I have a key called Promise that will open every door in this Doubting Castle."

At this he plucked it out, and followed by Hopeful, began to unfasten the big door of the dungeon.

The lock was very rusty and it required all Christian's strength to turn the key. At last the door was opened and creaked on its hinges.

The noise awakened the giant, who hastily made his way toward the prison. Hearing his heavy tread, the friends made for the main door of the castle. Quickly Christian inserted the wonderful Promise key and to their great relief the door yielded. Just then the giant bounded toward them, but in the moment of capture he had a fit and lay sprawled on the ground.

It was now morning and the sun was shining. The two pilgrims were able to find their way back to the stile, and getting on the Narrow Way, they made good progress for a few miles. Before they started the journey, however, they thanked their King for such a wonderful deliverance.

"Let us make a pillar and engrave a warning to other pilgrims who come this way," suggested Christian.

They found a suitable rock and carved the following inscription:

102

"Take heed to our warning, all you who pass by.
This ground is forbidden—take care!
Remember the straight Way will lead to the sky.
This meadow will lead to DESPAIR."

Having set the stone at the side of the Way, close to the stile, the pilgrims hoped that many people would be persuaded not to venture over.

The road began to ascend fairly steeply, but Christian and Hopeful found the path comfortable and they journeyed on without much difficulty.

All around the countryside was very beautiful with orchards, vineyards, and fountains of water. The mountains that surrounded the friends were called Delectable, and many shepherds were gazing their sheep on the side of the Way.

"Can you tell us who owns these wonderful estates?" Christian asked of the shepherds.

"Yes, we are employed by Emmanuel, who owns these beautiful hills. The sheep are His also, and He laid down His Life for them."

"Would you like to be shown around the estates?" asked one of the shepherds of the pilgrims.

"Yes, very much," replied Hopeful. "Is it possible to see the Celestial City from here?"

"Only on the far horizon can the Heavenly Land be viewed. It will be necessary to look through a special glass, and then all that you will be able to see will be the gate and some of its glory."

The shepherd showed them many wonderful scenes as

they looked down upon the land beneath. Being so high up, it was possible to see many places that they had visited on their journey. Doubting Castle could clearly be seen and also the stile over which they had ventured.

Their food was plentiful, for they ate the pleasant fruit that they found in the orchards and vineyards. For refreshment there were the fountains of living water, cool and clear.

"Could we borrow the glass in order to see yonder fair City?" Hopeful asked the shepherds. "We will be content to catch a glimpse of the Heavenly Shore, be it ever so faint!"

The shepherds agreed and said: "It will be necessary to climb this hill called Clear, and when we reach the summit you can both gaze to your hearts' content." Thus they led the pilgrims up the mountain.

Hopeful carefully took the instrument and, adjusting his sight, looked longingly toward the Celestial City.

"I can see the golden gates dimly," he exclaimed. "Perhaps you would like to use the glass, Christian?"

His friend readily consented, and he too could just make out a part of the City, but was unable to distinguish it.

"I see through a glass darkly," he cried, "but then face to face."

The time soon came for the pilgrims to leave the Delectable Mountains; so, bidding the shepherds farewell and thanking them for their great kindness, they walked downward until level ground was reached.

A little to the left of the road was a country called Conceit, and a very crooked path connected this area with the Narrow Way.

The shepherds on the Delectable Mountains.

At the junction of this crooked path stood a man whose name was Ignorance, and Christian asked him where he was going.

"Sir, I was born in the country called Conceit and am bound for the Celestial City."

"Are you sure that you will be admitted when you arrive there?" asked Christian.

"Yes, I think so, for I have been a very good fellow, paying all my debts, praying to God, going without food, paying money to the church, and giving to poor people who are in need."

"But you did not enter the Way by the lodge-gate, and therefore missed the Cross," replied Christian. "It is not possible to gain entrance into the City without coming that way."

"Gentlemen, you are utter strangers to me and I do not know you at all. Be content to follow your religion and I will follow mine. What does it matter if I came into the right road by means of the crooked path? I am here and mean to try by my good works to enter the Celestial City."

Christian turned to Hopeful and suggested that they walk ahead, for it was not possible to enjoy a conversation with one so conceited.

He added the wise words, "There is a way that seems right to a man, but the end of it brings destruction. Our King has said, 'I am the Way, the Truth, and the Life; no man comes to My Father but by Me.'"

TWELVE

The two pilgrims left Ignorance to walk behind, and they entered into an interesting conversation about a man called Little-faith who, though he was attacked by three ruffians, managed to reach the Celestial City.

The ruffians had robbed Little-faith of his money but failed to find his jewels or his scroll. Although his faith was small, it was sufficient to gain him an entrance into the Eternal Home.

"Which way shall we take?" asked Hopeful, for they had reached a part of the road where it divided. Just then a smooth-talking man dressed in a white robe came along and directed the pilgrims into a path that was slightly out of the Way. At first they thought that this was the Way, but after a while the track turned and their backs were toward the Celestial City.

The man very cunningly spread a net in front of them, and not looking where they were going, Christian and Hopeful became entangled in it. Try as they would the net would not break, and the man left them to their fate. How long they would have remained there no one could tell, but fortunately a kind-looking gentleman came along the road and helped them out of the net.

"Why were you so far off the Narrow Way?" he asked.

"We came to a place where the road forked and, forgetting to read our map, were led astray by a man who eventually entangled us in this snare." Christian went on to describe the man and his white robe.

"This man is called the Flatterer, and you should have known that what he told you was untrue." The stranger directed them on to the Narrow Way, advising them to beware of flatterers.

"Who is that man coming toward us, with his back toward Zion?" said Hopeful. "Let us ask his name."

"My name is Atheist," the man told the pilgrims. "Where are you going?"

"We are going to the Celestial City—to dwell there forever," said Christian.

"Don't make me laugh!" cried the man. "There is no such place."

"Oh, there is—for we have viewed it from the Delectable Mountains, and beside all this we have our scrolls that are to be handed in at the door." Hopeful was amazed to hear Atheist say that Heaven did not exist.

"This man is blinded by the god of this world," exclaimed Christian, and they both turned away from him, continuing their journey.

"Do you feel sleepy?" Hopeful asked his companion. "I feel very tired and should like to lie down and rest."

"No, my brother," counseled Christian. "This place is called the Enchanted Ground, and if we sleep here we may never wake. Let us watch and be sober. It would be good to talk about our past adventures so that we can keep ourselves awake.''

''Shall I tell you about my early life in Vanity Fair?'' suggested Hopeful.

''By all means. I shall be very interested in your story,'' said Christian.

''When I was quite young I enjoyed the pleasures to be found in the Fair and was no different from other boys. No one would have called me wicked, but as I grew older the simple things no longer interested me. The coarser people became my companions and we delighted in wrongdoing such as rioting, reveling, drinking, swearing, and telling lies. I continued with this kind of life until Faithful and you came to our town. When I saw how you behaved amid a people who were wicked and deceitful, my conscience began to trouble me and I learned about your King and the Celestial City. At first I tried doing good and going to church, but this did not make me feel better. I thought that by giving to the poor and being kind to the weak, your King would forgive me and take me to His Home on high. It was then that I learned about God and found that He hated evil doing, and that He would not accept my trying to live a clean life. You see, I had forgotten about my past wrongdoing and foolishly thought that God would overlook that because I was now a better man.''

''What did you do then?'' asked Christian.

''I could do nothing to earn my way to the Celestial City, for all that I had done was not good enough. Then it was that I learned about God's Son, who came from Heaven and died for sinners—thus paying the penalty that was really mine. I understood that He had earned for me my entrance into Heaven.''

''Did you thank Him for dying on the Cross?'' asked Christian.

''Yes indeed,'' replied Hopeful, ''and just as you saw the Cross on the little hill—so did I. Although no one saw my burden, yet it had been there until it was removed from me at that holy place. My heart was then filled with joy at the knowledge of being forgiven, and I sang this little song:

> ''On the Cross my Saviour died,
> For my sins was crucified;
> I can sing for I am free;
> He has now accepted me.''

Their conversation proved to be so engrossing that the Enchanted Ground was soon passed and they now came to the Land of Beulah.

The air here was very sweet, for it was filled with the scent of many flowers. Birds were singing in the trees and the two pilgrims were filled with rapture as they realized that their journey was nearly finished. The sun shone all the time, warming them with its pleasant rays, and they were beyond the reach of all their enemies. From Beulah Land the two friends could clearly see the Celestial City, and the glory of the place was beyond description.

Doubting Castle was now far away and they were safe from the clutches of Giant Despair.

They stayed in Beulah Land for a time and rested their

weary bodies. The fruit of the trees was delicious, and although they ate a great amount they did not tire of it. Shining ones who came from the City spoke with them, telling them more of the wonders to be seen over the river.

"Is there a river to cross?" asked Christian.

"Yes, can you not see it winding in the valley?" An angel was pointing toward the west. "It divides the Land of Beulah from the Heavenly Shore, and you must go through it to reach the other side."

At this Christian was afraid and wondered how he would be able to ford it. Hopeful, however, encouraged him and reminded his friend of the many difficult places that they had overcome during the long journey. "Surely the King will help us now after having guided us thus far," he said.

"You are right. I must trust and not be afraid."

The time came for them to depart from Beulah Land, so they prepared themselves and walked toward the river. It looked dark and forbidding, but without much hesitation they waded into the water and moved toward the farther shore.

Christian, however, began to sink and cried in his distress: "I sink in deep waters; the billows go over my head; all the waves go over me!"

He thought that he would never reach the other side.

Hopeful remained true to his name, and lifting his eyes toward the City saw two shining angels waiting at the gate to receive them.

"Be of good courage, my dear friend. I can feel the bottom of the stream and am able to walk."

Christian could not be comforted and was unable to see the

shore. Presently he brightened up and said: "When I pass through the waters, my King is with me and He will not let me be drowned."

At this he too was able to feel the bottom and made an effort to walk upright. It had now become shallower, and as they reached the Heavenly shore the two angels came toward them, helping them up the bank.

Having reached dry land, they were conducted up the hill, on top of which stood the Celestial City, shining as a bright jewel.

Their garments, including Christian's armor, had been left in the river, for there was no need to wear mortal dress any more. Although the climb was steep, they had strength to mount upward, the angels helping them all the time.

"When you come into the City through the gate, white robes will be given you and crowns of gold placed upon your heads. Then you will see the King in all His beauty and you will serve Him forever." Thus spoke one of the shining ones.

Soon the gate loomed in sight and a great company of the heavenly host came out to meet them. After messages of welcome, the pilgrims were asked to hand over the scrolls that they had received at the Cross, and one of the angels turned them over to a messenger who proceeded to the Palace. He was received by the King and asked to wait while the scrolls were read.

"Where are the men?" asked their Lord.

The messenger replied that they were waiting at the gate for admittance.

"Go and tell the angels to escort My faithful servants into

Christian and Hopeful entering the Celestial City.

the City and bring them to Me."

The messenger lost no time, but swiftly returned to the company who, on hearing the King's request, clothed the two pilgrims in shining white robes and placed jeweled crowns upon their heads.

As they entered the City, the faces of Christian and Hopeful became transfigured and they shone like the sun. The streets of the beautiful place were paved with gold, and on reaching the Palace the lovely music played on harps and viols sounded loud and clear.

The angels conducted them into the Presence of the King, and as they approached the throne they fell down on their faces and worshiped.

"Well done, good and faithful servants; enter into the joy of your Lord."

What a wonderful welcome for poor pilgrims from the City of Destruction! As they rose from their knees the King smiled a sweet smile and bade them be joyful forevermore.

It is not possible to recount all that happened in that realm of joy, but it is certain that Christian and Hopeful were nevermore sad; nor did they cry, for the Lord wiped away all tears from their eyes. They served Him continually, and the song that was ever on their lips was:

"Unto Him who has loved us and washed us from sin,
Unto Him be the glory forever. Amen."